FOR PK

With many thanks to Emma and Jenny at Hodder,
and Caroline at David Higham.

HODDER CHILDREN'S BOOKS
First published in Great Britain in 2017 by Hodder Children's Books

Copyright © Fiona Roberton, 2017

The moral rights of the author have been asserted.
All rights reserved

A CIP catalogue record for this book is available from the British Library.

HB: 978 1 444 93724 4
PB: 978 1 444 93726 8

10 9 8 7 6 5 4 3 2 1

Printed and bound in China

MIX
Paper from
responsible sources
FSC® C104740
FSC
www.fsc.org

Hodder Children's Books, an imprint of Hachette Children's Group, part of Hodder and Stoughton,
Carmelite House, 50 Victoria Embankment, London, EC4Y 0DZ

An Hachette UK Company
www.hachette.co.uk
www.hachettechildrens.co.uk

SWAPSIES

Fiona Roberton

Fang loves Sock.

Sock is **yellow**.

Sock is **stripey**.

Sock is **squeezy**.

Sock smells like **bananas**.

Sock is **amazing**.

"I love you Sock,"
says Fang.

But look!
Here comes Philip.

Philip has **his** favourite
toy with him too.

Train is **red**.

Train is **shiny**.

Train is **honky**.

HONK!
HONK!

Train smells like **tomatoes**.

Train is **magnificent**.

"Train looks like **lots** of fun
to play with," says Fang.

"**Much** more fun than Sock."

"**Swapsies?**" suggests Fang.

"**Yes please!**" says Philip, because
Philip is **very** good at sharing.

"I love you Train,"
says Fang.

But look!
Here comes Simon.

Simon has **his** favourite
toy with him too.

Ball is **blue.**

Ball is **round.**

Ball is **bouncy.**

Ball smells like **chocolate chip cookies.**

Ball is **spectacular.**

"Ball looks **very** fun to play with," says Fang.

"Even **more** fun than Train **and** Sock."

"**Swapsies?**" suggests Fang.

"**Okay!**" says Simon, because Simon
would really like to play with Train.

HONK!

HONK!

"I love you Ball,"
says Fang.

"You are the most **spectacular** toy in the whole wide..."

Fang is missing Ball.

But he is **really** missing Sock.

But look!
Here comes Philip,

and here comes Simon.
Simon still has Train,
and Philip still has Sock!

"What happened to Ball?"
asks Simon.

"Ball is no longer with us," says Fang.

"But look!" he says. "I found Stick.
Stick is brown and smells like wet dog.
Stick is **fantastic,**" he tells Philip.

"**Swapsies?**" suggests Fang.

"**Yes please!**" says Philip, because Philip
really is very, **very** good at sharing.

Sock and Fang, Fang and Sock,
back together, forever and ever.
"I **love** you Sock," says Fang.

"I will **never** swap you again,
for any other...

...toy!"